KB127066

여기 그대 곁에

꽃 한송이 피었어요

A small flower has bloomed here beside you

여기 그대 곁에

펴낸곳 (주)도어스
지은이 강영희
그린이 이성표
디자인 조의환
펴낸이 김동규
초판1쇄 2017년 4월 11일
주소 03169 서울 종로구 사직로10길 7(내자동)
전화 070-4231-4232
Facebook 강영희
Twitter @gumunjadab
Instagram kang_younghee_love
홈페이지 9moon.co.kr
등록번호 2016년 5월 12일 제300-2016-54호
ISBN 979-11-958208-3-2
값 13,000원

여기 그대 곁에
꽃 한송이 피었어요

A small flower has bloomed here beside you

강영희 글 | 이성표 그림

번역 Translation

Mi Na Sketchley

Korean Translator & Conference Interpreter

MA MCIL DPSI Korean (English Law) NRPSI

Reading for DPhil Oriental Studies, Oriental Studies

Faculty, University of Oxford

Anthony Charles E. Banks

Editor and proofreader. ESL professional

University of London

Hyangkue Lee

Independent Researcher, Writer and Translator

PhD. Education, Seoul National University

차례 Contents

9 마지막 사랑 the last of love

23 아름다운 배암 a gorgeous snake

33 송이송이 눈꽃송이 flake, flake, snowflake

49 꽃 한송이 a blooming flower

63 손을 잡아주세요 hold my hand

77 무지개 a rainbow

89 연미복을 입은 베짱이 a penguin suited grasshopper

101 고래 a whale

115 창가에 앉아 by the window

129 큰 사람 a gigantic person

141 오래 기다렸어요 I waited so long for you

마지막 사랑

the last of love

세월호

인천에서 제주를 오가는 6,825톤의 여객선.
2014년 4월 16일 알 수 없는 원인에 의해
침몰하여, 수학여행을 가고 있던 고등학생
250명을 포함한 304명이 사망하였다.
유가족들과 국민들의 3년간의 촛불 시위는
박근혜, 최순실 게이트를 밝히는 시발이
되었으며, 대통령 박근혜는 2017년 3월 10일
파면되었다.

Sewol Ferry

The Sewol Ferry was a 6,825-ton vessel,
which used to travel between Incheon and
Jeju. The sinking of the Sewol occurred on
the 16th April 2014 due to unknown causes
and 304 passengers, including 250 secondary
school students, who had set off on a school
trip, died in the disaster. The 3 year long
candlelight vigil, led by the victims' families
and the Korean nation, triggered the 'Park
Geun-hye-Choi Soon-sil gate' scandal and
President Park Geun-hye was impeached on
10th March 2017.

세월호에 마지막 사랑이 타고 있었나봐

아이들 곁에 사랑도 있었나봐

사랑 생각만 하면 머릿속이 하얘지고 아이들이 생각나니 말야

아이들이랑 사랑이랑 아직도 바닷속에 있으니 말야

어쩌면 좋아

우리 다시는 사랑할 수 없을지도 모르잖아

Perhaps the last kind of love was on board the *Sewol Ferry*

Perhaps it resided there, next to the kids

because whenever I think about love, my mind goes blank

and the kids in the ferry appear

because the kids and love are still at the bottom of the sea

Oh, dear, what should we do?

We may never love again.

문 두드려요 쾅쾅 문 두드려요

문 부여잡고 콰앙 문이 되어요

뒤집힌 문이 말해요

닫힌 문이 사랑을 말해요

왜 사랑하지 않았냐고

왜 사랑 아닌 거짓을 말하고 있냐고

왜 아직도 사랑이 아니냐고

Bang! Bang! They are pounding on the doors

Holding onto the doors, Clang!

They have now become doors themselves

The upside-down door and the locked door say of love,

"Why didn't you love us?",

"Why are you still telling lies, not speaking of love?",

"Why is it not love yet?"

어디로 간 거니

다시 만날 수 없는 거니

울어도 눈물이 마르지 않아

세월이 흘러도 달라지지 않아

눈물이 나를 삼켜서

몸뚱이가 흐물거려 물이 되려나 봐

벌써 물이 된 거니

바다가 되어 있는 거니

바다보다 큰 사랑이 되어야

만날 수 있는 거니

Where have you gone?

Can't I see you again?

My tears are not drying up

Nothing has changed, even after all this time

My body is all wobbly as the tears consume me

Perhaps I am turning into water?

Have I already become water?

Have I already become an ocean?

Do I need to become a love which is bigger than an ocean?

Would I see you then?

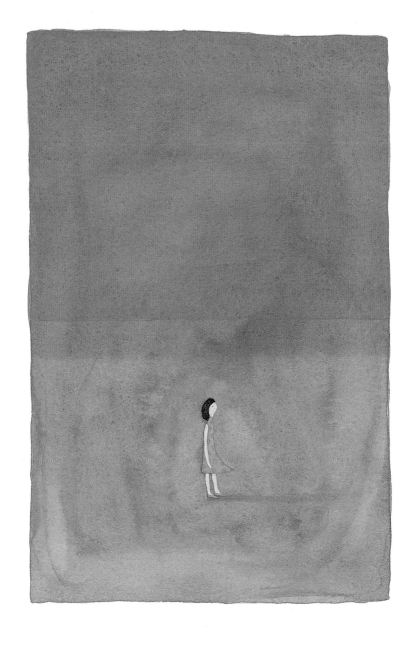

얼마나 무서웠을까

얼마나 무서웠을까

얼마나 무서웠을까

얼마나 무서웠을까

얼마나 무서웠을까

얼마나 무서웠을까

도무지 알 길이 없네

그러므로 이제 나는 사랑을 모르네

사랑으로 갈 길이 없네

It must have been so scary,

it must have been so scary,

it must have been so scary,

it must have been so scary,

it must have been so scary,

it must have been so scary

No one will ever know

Hence, I do not know what love is anymore

There is now no path to love.

구렁이 한 마리 기어가요

고개 돌리고 눈 감으니 덜컥 품 속으로 파고 들어요

왈칵 눈물이 흐르네요

옛 사랑이 슬픈 구렁이 되어 뒤따라 오다니요

제발 부디 구렁이의 몸을 벗고

옛날 옛적의 아름다운 당신으로 환생하시길요

A python is slithering

I turn my head away and close my eyes,

and it suddenly slips into my arms I burst into tears

How could my old love turn into a sad python and slink behind me?

Please strip off the python's body and become reborn, back to who you were

the beautiful one you once were

세월이 흘러도 흐르지 못하는 것이 있어요

하늘이 천 개의 손을 내어 세상의 마음을 천 갈래로 찢어요

천 줄기의 눈물이 우릉우릉 울돌목으로 모여요

바다의 울음소리에 귀 기울인 이순신 장군처럼

우리, 명량대첩을 승리로 이끌 거예요

There are certain things that fail to flow even when time passes

The skies stick out a thousand hands and they rip up the world's mind

into a thousand threads

The stems of a thousand tears gather into *Ul-Dol-Mok*

We shall achieve a victory in the *Battle of Myeongnyang* – just as Admiral

Yi Sun-sin did, who listened to the bawling of the sea.

이순신

1545~1598. 조선 중기의 명장. 해군 제독. 1592년
임진왜란이 발발하자, 탁월한 전법을 구사하고
거북선을 제조하여 왜군을 물리쳤다. 1597년의
명량해전은 전세를 역전시켜 제해권을 되찾은
전설적인 대첩이다. (명량의 순우리말이 울돌목이다.)
시호인 충무(忠武)를 따라, 흔히 충무공으로 불린다.

Admiral Yi Sun-sin (1545-1598) was a great
naval commander in the *Joseon Dynasty*. When
the Imjin war broke out in 1592, he defeated
the Japanese navy by resurrecting the Turtle
Ship (also known as the *Geobukseon*) with his
tactical genius. The Battle of Myungnyang circa
1597 is regarded as one of the most legendary
battles in Korea as it dramatically turned the tide
of the war and returned the rule of the sea to
Korea. *'Uldolmok'* is the pure Korean word for
'Myungnyang'. Chungmu gong is the commonly
used appellation for Admiral *Yi Sun-sin* which is
from his posthumous name *Chungmu.*

당신은 해당화 피기 전에 오신다고 하였습니다
뒷동산에 해당화 피었다고 다투어 말하기로 못들은 체 하였더니
봄바람은 나는 꽃을 불어 경대 위에 놓입니다
꽃은 눈물에 비쳐 둘도 되고 셋도 됩니다
당신은 해당화 지기 전에 오셔야 합니다

You promised to return before the sweetbriers bloom
As I tried hard to ignore the constant nattering about the now blooming
sweetbriers, the spring breeze brings a bloomed flower onto my dresser
This single flower becomes two, then three when seen through my teary eyes
You must come back before the sweetbriers wither away.

아름다운 배암

a gorgeous snake

꼿꼿한 목을 높이 세우고 아름다운 배암 하나 내 집으로 왔어요

붉은 입설을 곱게 다문 자랑찬 얼굴이었어요

내 몸으로 오는 배암이 기뻤어요

몸돌려 배암을 안는 순간 털썩 허물이 떨어졌어요

사랑의 손길이 다음 생의 문을 활짝 열었어요

Holding her neck upright, a gorgeous snake entered my house

She had a boastful face with her ruddy lips firmly closed

I was delighted to see the snake heading to me

As I turned and embraced the snake, her slough fell down

The hand of love opens the door wide to the next life.

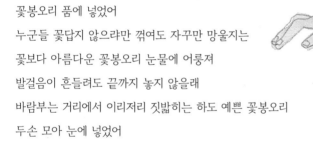

꽃봉오리 품에 넣었어

누군들 꽃답지 않으랴만 꺾여도 자꾸만 망울지는

꽃보다 아름다운 꽃봉오리 눈물에 어룽져

발걸음이 흔들려도 끝까지 놓지 않을래

바람부는 거리에서 이리저리 짓밟히는 하도 예쁜 꽃봉오리

두손 모아 눈에 넣었어

I hold a bud close

Of course all the flowers are flowery but the bud is prettier,

as it doesn't constantly bear buds after being plucked as flowers do

I won't let you go, bud, even though I tremble at the tears of your allure

The sheer beauty of the bud, trampled over here and there in the windy street

 I gather you in my hands and put you in my eyes.

아름다운 뱀

a gorgeous snake

2-3

밥 한 그릇 앞에 놓고 눈물 흘렸어
밥 한 그릇의 위로를 잊고 살았지
입 언저리에 밥풀 묻히며
눈물도 한데 넘겼어
흐득이는 가을비가 덜컹 창문을 치고 지나가도
당신이 차려준 밥상은 끄떡없이 내 앞에 있어 다행이에요
그래 참 다행이야

I shed tears before a bowl of steamed rice

I had forgotten the comfort a bowl of steamed rice offers

A grain of rice is stuck on my lip

I swallow it, crying

I am glad the table you prepared is not budging an inch

despite the autumn rain rattling the windows

I am so very grateful for such simple mercies.

A clean-eyed deer rushed to me, snuggling into my arms

We all started to get invaded with these shameful thoughts

The deer-like love appears as a mirage and vanishes as a mirage

Such a love teaches us that you, I and the world are all only one entity

Then it disappears somewhere.

맑은 눈동자를 가진 사슴이 다급히 뛰어와요 다짜고짜 품으로 파고 들어요

부끄러운 생각이 너도 나도 들어요

사슴을 닮은 사랑이 신기루처럼 나타났다 신기루처럼 사라져요

그런 사랑이 너랑 나랑 우주랑 하나임을 알려주고

어디론가 사라져요

송이송이 눈꽃송이

flake, flake, snowflake

송이송이 눈꽃송이 하얀 꽃송이
하늘에서 내려오는 하얀 꽃송이
나무에도 들판에도 동구 밖에도
골고루 나부끼네 아름다워라
송이송이 눈꽃송이 하얀 꽃송이
천지에 가득한 하얀 꽃송이
거리에도 골목에도 마음 속에도
골고루 나부끼네
아름다워라

Flake, flake, snowflake, white flower-flake

White flakes coming from the sky

On trees, on fields, even on the outskirts of a village

Fluttering everywhere, so evenly

How amazing

Flake, flake, snowflake, white flower-flake

White flakes filling Heaven and Earth

On streets, on alleys, even on hearts

Fluttering everywhere, so evenly

How amazing.

죽어버린 해님이 도로 살아나는 까닭을 난 알아요

누군가 해님을 사랑하기 때문이에요

캄캄한 그믐밤 홀로 일어나 어둔 하늘 보며

눈물로 소망하기 때문이에요

사랑으로 기원하기 때문이에요

보세요 두근거리는 젊은 새해가 다시 떠올라요

I know the reason why the once dead sun comes back alive

That's because someone loves the sun

That's because someone wakes up alone on a pitch black moonless night

and eagerly wishes for it, with tears, looking up to the dark sky

That's because someone prays for it with love

Look! A young sun, heart beating, rises again.

A spider said "There was a blessed weaver, she was so brilliant,

that she caused even a goddess to kneel."

"The goddess presented false virtue while the woman showed genuine

desire."

"I am now ready to kneel in front of her sanctity."

"I am now ready to express my respect in front of the cobweb,

under the sunlight."

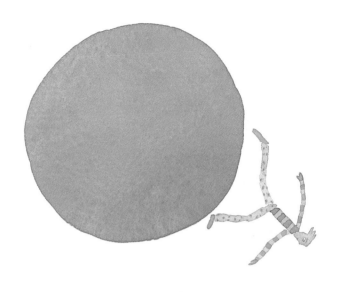

거미가 말했다네 베짜는 여인이 있었다네
여신조차 무릎을 꿇을 정도였다네
여신은 거짓 덕목을 말했고 여인은 진정한 욕망을 말했다네
이제 그녀의 성스러움 앞에 무릎 꿇을 작정이라네
햇살 아래 눈부신 거미줄 앞에 경의를 표할 생각이라네

불꽃을 닮은 화산의 아름다움을 예전엔 미처 몰랐어요

아득한 옛적 땅 속 마그마의 폭발이 눈앞에 보여요

끓어오르는 용암 속으로 뛰어들고 싶어요

굳어버린 산이 되어도 영원히 잠들지 않는 법을

당신이 가르쳐 주셨거든요

I never fully grasped the beauty of a volcano - resembling a searing flame

I see the eruption of magma which happened so long ago, deep in the earth

I want to dive into the seething lava

because you showed me how to stay awake eternally,

even after I turn into a rigid mountain.

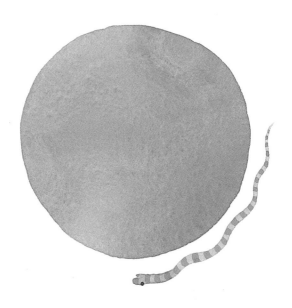

늦은 오후 햇살이 아직 허공에 걸려 있을 때
당신의 손에 이끌려 들판을 헤메고 다녔어
바로 여기야 찰칵
당신의 카메라가 사랑의 스냅을 찍었고
덜컹 해 떨어지는 소리 들려왔어
다행이야 따스한 사진 한 장 품 안에 남아 있거든

When the late-afternoon sunlight was still up in the air

Holding hands, you led me and we wandered all over the place in an open field

"This is it! Click!"

You created a snapshot of love and I heard

the heavy thump of the falling sun

How merciful, at least a warm shred of a photo remains with me.

불꽃 속으로 뛰어들었다구

세상에서 제일 아름다운 꽃이더라구

뜨겁지 않았냐구

불꽃의 꽃술은 차가운 이슬이더라구

가끔씩 몸부림쳤지만

불꽃이 몸을 뒤챌 때 나도 따라 몸을 뒤챈 거였다구

그렇게 불꽃 속에서 나도 몰래 죽음을 맞이했다구

I jumped into the flowery flame

It was the most beautiful flower in the whole world

Wasn't it scorching hot? Someone asked

Well, the pistil of the flame was cold dew

From time to time I found myself twisting and writhing,

but the truth is that I was just copying what the flame was doing

That's how I faced my death in the flowery flame,

even before I had noticed it.

당신 냄새가 좋아 강아지처럼 따라다니며 네가 말했어

강아지를 안아올리며 부비부비 냄새를 섞었지

사랑은 냄새를 나누는 거야

구석구석 수상한 냄새가 야릇한 향내로 변하는 거야

아득한 냄새에 취해 비틀거리는 거야

You told me once, "I like your scent",

as you chased after me like a little puppy

Picking up a puppy, our scents blended together

with the rubbing of our cheeks

"Love is all about sharing each other's scent,

about changing every part of a once suspicious scent into an alluring fragrance,

and about us staggering under its intoxicating scent."

이제 큰 소리로 말할 수 있어 한달음에 끝까지 다녀왔거든

지구 한 바퀴 돌고 왔거든 세월의 비밀을 눈동자에 새겨넣었거든

이제 작은 소리로 속삭일 거야

사랑으로 너를 안고 끝까지 살아갈 거야

삼백육십오 바퀴 사랑으로 돌고 돌 거야

I can now speak with full confidence having been to the end in a single bound,

having turned a full circle of the Earth, and having engraved the secret of time

in my eyes

I am now going to whisper

I am going to grab you in love and live until it ends

I am going to circumvent the three-hundred-and-sixty-five wheels of love

again and again.

I put on my shoes and hit the road

A tap tap tapping follows me like a puppy

The faster I walk, the higher the pup jumps and yelps

Wherever, whenever, I'm always on my way to you

Please wait

I am on my way now.

구두 신고 길을 나섰어

따각따각 발자국도 따라 나섰어 강아지처럼

나를 따라와 공연히 발걸음이 빨라져

강아지도 덩달아 뛰는 걸 올려다보며 멍멍 짓는 걸

언제 어디서나 너에게 가는 길이야

기다려요

지금 가는 중이야

꽃 한송이

a blooming flower

I could accept death because I have lived my life just as I have wanted to.

I could visit the other world since I have lived a full life

just like a blooming flower

As I was turning out from the end of the street,

a little flower was smiling at me

I emptied my pocket and gave her everything I had,

then I took my final breath

The curtain came down-this was done by love.

꽃 한 송이
a blooming flower
4-1

한 생애 마음껏 살았으니 죽어도 될 것 같았어

꽃 한송이 피우듯 아낌없이 살았으니 다른 세상으로 가보고 싶더라구

막다른 길 돌아나오는데 작은 꽃 하나 날 보고 웃더라니까

주머니 털어 녀석에게 주고 숨을 거두었어 사랑으로 막을 내렸어

꽃 한 송이
a blooming flower
4-2

The sound of cicada surges like giant waves

The cicada sound we meet at the end of the summer heat divulges

that it is time for one to withdraw as expected

The Bailiff of Time shall make sure that execution takes place

Thus, Aroint thee, hatred!

leave only the sweet love behind

Aroint thee, all hatred!

쓰르라미 소리가 집채만한 파도처럼 밀려온다
더위의 끄트머리에서 만나는 쓰르람 소리는
물러갈 것이 물러갈 것임을 알려준다
갈 것은 가리라 때의 집행관이 그렇게 하시리
그리하여 증오는 가라 향그러운 사랑만 남고
모오든 증오는 가라

I can happily die if I meet love like the sky and the ocean

People say that there is no such love,

but I am wandering around, to find it all by myself

I finally met you on the ninety ninth hill - the last one-

as I was falling down and tumbling over

Now I will die, burying my face in your bosom.

하늘 같고 바다 같은 그런 사랑 만나면 죽어도 좋겠네

그런 사랑 없다고 모두들 말하지만

그런 사랑 찾아 나홀로 헤매네

아흔아홉고개 마지막 고개에서

넘어지고 뒹굴다 당신을 만났네

당신 가슴에 얼굴을 묻고 이제 그만 죽으려네

It was indeed a deep lake

Something floated to the surface

It was a long-legged pond skater

A fit of pique floated too

I scooped up the pond skater with a net

The clamorous bobbing calmed and the lake once again

became deep and still

I walked into the lake

It was indeed a tranquil lake.

깊은 호수였어 호수

표면에 무언가 떠올랐어

다리가 긴 소금쟁이였어

어처구니 없는 분노도 떠올랐어

긴 뜰채로 소금쟁이를 건져 올렸어

시끄러운 일렁임은 조용해졌고

호수는 다시 깊어졌어

호수 속으로 걸어 들어갔어

깊은 호수였어

병아리떼 쫑쫑쫑 놀고간 뒤에
미나리 파란싹이 돋아났어요
요것 보세요
제 마음 복판에 미나리깡 하나 만들었어요
어지러운 논물에서 거머리 떼어내며 자라는 미나리들처럼
연한 마음싹을 자꾸만 베어내어 당신께 드리려구요
이리와 요것 보세요

A little green dropwort bud popped out

after a brood of chicks had played and left

Look at this!

I made a dropwort bed in the centre of my heart

Just like the dropwort buds grow, by peeling leeches off them,

I am going to cut off the delicate buds of my heart and give them to you

Please come and have a look at this.

기다릴께 걱정 말고 다녀와

환한 가을꽃 되어 돌아올 거지

옹그라진 맨드라미 되어 돌아올 거지

진자주빛 다알리아 되어 돌아올 거지

한숨 소리에 놀라 가을이 가버리지 않도록

말없이 널 기다릴께 언제나 이 자리에서 기다릴께

Don't worry, I will wait for you

I'll see you soon

You'll return as a bright autumn flower,

as a curled-up cockscomb or a red-violet dahlia

I will wait for you in silence so that the autumn won't be frightened away

by my deep sigh

I will be waiting for you, right here as always.

거울 속의 아이가 말했어

지난 생은 잊었어요

까만 눈동자를 빛내며 아이가 말했어

이번 생을 다시 시작해요

기쁨으로 가득한 생애가 완성될 거예요

아이는 거울 속으로 사라졌고 나도 따라 사라졌어

거울 속의 아이가 새로운 시간의 주인이야

A child inside a mirror told me

"I've forgotten about my past life"

With his dark eyes gleaming, he said

"I'll start this life again"

"I'm sure it will be a life full of joy"

The boy vanished into the mirror as did I

The boy in the mirror is the master of this newly conjured time.

비가 와요 주룩주룩 가슴 속에도 와요

허둥지둥 작아져 주먹 속으로 들어가요

주먹을 펴보니 편지가 있네요 당신이 보내셨군요

가을비 내리고 겨울눈 몰아치면 봄꽃 필 거라 하시네요

편지를 활짝 펼치니 환한 복사꽃 그늘이 아스라해요

It's raining, streaming down into my heart too

In a hustle and bustle, my heart becomes smaller and seeps into my fist

I open my clenched hand and there is a letter from you

It says that once the autumn rain has fallen and the gust of winter snow has

gone, spring flowers will bloom

Fully unfolding the letter, the shade of the bright peach blossom becomes

hazy.

손을 잡아주세요

hold my hand

손을 잡아주세요 손가락도 잡을래요

새끼 손가락은 돌돌 감을까요

손이 따뜻해요

우리 이겨낼 수 있겠죠

그럴 수 있겠죠

손을 잡아주세요

손바닥도 마주칠래요

손이 있어 다른 손을 그리워 하는 건 기쁜 일이네요

당신 손이 참 따뜻해요

Hold my hand, and my fingers too

Roll, roll, shall we coil around our baby fingers?

These hands are so warm

"Will we be able to overcome this?"

We can of course, right?

Hold my hand

And hold our palms together too

It's marvellous that we have hands that allow us to yearn for other hands

Your hands are so very warm.

손을 잡아주세요
hold my hand
5-1

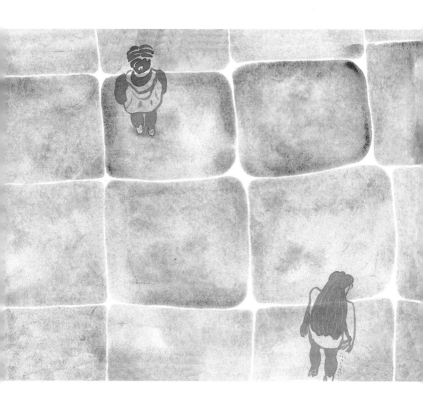

새벽녘 꿈길에서 너를 만났어

뛰어가 반가운 말 하려는데 말이 나오지 않았어

하늘땅이 와르르 무너진달까

꿀먹은 벙어리처럼 말이 나오지 않았어

눈감고 팔벌려 너를 안았어

첫사랑처럼 가슴에 안았어

I encountered you in a dream at dawn

I ran to you to say hello, but I couldn't utter a word

It felt like the sky had fallen in on me

No words came out as if I were rendered mute

Closing my eyes and stretching out my arms,

I hugged you just like it was my first love.

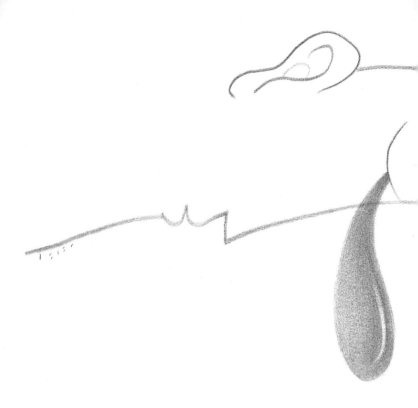

Life sometimes becomes lively with a song of a person who shall not be forgotten

The evanescent singer comes alive and sings a song that had been forgotten

"My darling, rankled in my heart, don't forget me"

Without his song, life is like a river with no vestige

I always look forward to having you

Don't ever forget me.

삶은 잊지 말아야 할 사람의 노래로 가끔씩 수런거리네

사라진 사람이 되살아나 잊혀진 노래를 부르네

날 잊지 말아요 내 밤에 맺힌 그대여

그의 노래가 아니라면 삶은 자취없는 강물과 다르지 않다네

나 항상 너를 고대하노라

날 잊지 말아요

호랑나비를 보았어 숲속 꽃밭에서 보았어

자세히 보니 키 큰 남자더라구

남자가 웃으며 말했어 멀리 다녀오느라 수고가 많았어

멋진 남자더라구

당신 말이야 어젯밤 꿈에 숲속 꽃밭에 가지 않았어

거기서 근사한 호랑나비를 만나지 않았어

I saw a swallowtail in a flower bed inside the forest

I looked closely and realised that it was a tall man

He smiled and said "You must be tired from such a long journey."

He was a dapper gentleman

"Didn't you visit a flower bed in your dreams last night?"

"Didn't you meet a splendid swallowtail there?".

네 눈 속을 보았더니 거울같은 눈동자 속에 내가 있는 거야

도망치듯 눈을 감았더니

내 눈 속에 또 네가 있는 거야 칠흙같은 눈동자 속을 환히 비추는 거야

눈부셔 다시 눈을 떴더니 태양같은 네가 가로막는 거야

너에게 사로잡혔어

As I looked into your eyes, I saw myself mirrored in your iris

Closing my eyes, as if to escape

I found you inside my eyes again, shining through my pitch-black iris

Opening my eyes again because of the dazzling light, you, as bright as the

sun, blocked my escape

I am captured by you.

울고 싶었어 울음이 터질 것 같아 입을 다물었어

울그락 불그락

화난 얼굴이 되어버렸어

한방울의 눈물도 흘리지 않았어

희뿌연 눈앞에서 흐느끼는 네가 보여

사랑은 울면 안되는 걸 알아

내 울음을 네 눈물로 허락하는 게 사랑인 걸 알아

I really wanted to cry but I kept my mouth tightly shut

Otherwise I would have burst into tears

My face reddened as if I were angry

I didn't shed a single tear

I can see you sobbing through these hazy eyes

I know love wasn't something to be cried over

It is all about letting your crying flow into my tears.

늑대 한 마리 광야에서 만났어

회색빛 털을 가진 늑대였어

사나웠지만 눈빛이 따뜻했어

앞발을 들고 서럽게 울길래 나도 따라 목놓아 울었어

황폐한 세상 기막힌 세상에서 으르렁 그르렁 나라를 세웠어

잿빛 벌판에서 새나라를 세웠어

I met a wolf in the wilderness

It was a wolf with grey fur

He was vicious and wild, yet had warmth in his eyes

At his sad howling, I too wept bitterly

Growling and snarling – we built a nation in this devastated world, in this

absurd world

We built a new nation in this ashy wilderness.

밤송이 하나 품에 안았지

고슴도치 마냥 웅크리고 있더군

모른 척 꽈악 안았지

어이쿠야 피흘릴 줄 알았는데

어이쿠야 눈물이 흐르더군

어쩔 줄 몰라 하며 파고 들더군

어쩔 줄 몰라 하며 세게 안았지 밤송이 하나 품에 안았지

I held a chestnut burr in my arms

It was crouching there like a hedgehog

I hugged it hard pretending not to notice it

My goodness I thought I would bleed

But no! I found myself weeping

Not knowing what else to do, it crawled deeper into me

Equally flustered, I held it tighter in my arms.

무지개

a rainbow

무지개를 보았어 내 생애 다시는 만날 것 같지 않은 무지개였어

무지개는 사라졌고 세상은 다시 평범해졌어

네가 나타나 말했지 무지개를 보았냐고

퀭한 눈으로 너를 보았어

작은 무지개가 눈 앞에 걸려 있었지

황홀한 눈으로 너를 보았어

I saw a rainbow which I am unlikely to ever meet again in my lifetime

It disappeared and the world became featureless again

You appeared and asked me if I had seen the rainbow

I looked back at you with these sunken eyes of mine

A little rainbow was there before me

I saw you with these eyes of mine, full of rapture.

A scarecrow drifted here

The sparrows all flew down, chattered then blenchingly flew away

I wanted to follow too

But thinking of you, I held out my hand

'Pop!' The scarecrow vanished, leaving only a single teardrop behind

The sparrows are chit-chatting again

"What was that?"

"It was a petrifying scarecrow!"

허수아비 하나 바람에 날아왔어

참새들이 날아와 재잘거리다 흠칫 날아갔어

나도 날아가려다

당신을 떠올리며 손을 내밀었지

펑 하고 허수아비 날아간 자리에 눈물 한 방울 남았어

참새들이 다시 재잘거리네

뭐였을까

정말 무서운 허수아비였어

I met a kid who possessed a pleasing scent

Led by the scent, I hugged him

The little boy said

"I smelt something alluring."

To which I said "We have now shared this scent, the far-off day's promise is complete."

The little boy laughed over and over again.

아이를 만났어 좋은 향기를 가진 아이였어

향기에 이끌려 아이를 안았어

품 속의 아이가 말했어

좋은 향기를 맡았어요

이제 향기를 나누었으니 까마득한 약속이 이루어진 거란다

아이가 웃었어 자꾸만 웃었어

작은 꽃 한송이 수줍게 피었어요

어쩐지 수줍어 발간 얼굴로 보았어요

꽃이 말했어요 당신처럼 예쁜 꽃은 처음 만났어요

꽃이 저보고 꽃이라고 말했어요

그래서 알게 되었어요 저도 꽃이라는 걸 말이에요

당신이 저를 꽃으로 변하게 하셨어요

A small cluster of flowers bloomed shyly

I looked at the flower with shyness in my countenance

The flower uttered "I have never met a flower like you, how pretty!"

The flower told me that I am a flower

That's how I got to know that I am one of them too

Darling, you transformed me into a flower.

목화 한 송이 품에 안아요

목화 따라 나도 벙글어요

얼굴을 묻으며 그녀를 안아요

구름 같은 목화를 안아요

가만히 몸을 섞으려는데 목화가 말해요

슬픔에서 기쁨까지 당신을 안고 있을래요

조용히 마음을 놓아요

I hug a stem of cotton

A gentle smile beams from me, just like the cotton

Putting my face down on her, I hug her

I embrace the cloudlike cotton

As I try to snuggle into her softly, the cotton utters

"I will hold and keep you in sadness and in joy."

I rest my mind in peace.

무지개

a rainbow

6-6

일곱 명의 난장이가 일곱 개의 사과를 들고 궁전 문을 두드려요

백설공주는 거울을 들여다보고 있어요

거울 속에는 무서운 계모가 있어요

백설공주는 사과를 먹고 영원한 잠에 빠져야 해요

거울 속에는 일곱 명의 현자가 있어요

The seven dwarfs, holding seven apples, were knocking on the palace gate

Snow White is looking in the mirror

There is a horrible stepmother inside the mirror

Snow White must fall into a deep slumber after biting a poisonous apple

There are seven wise men inside the mirror.

가을비 뿌리는 아침

이리저리 몸을 뒤척이니 따라 뒤척이는 것들이 있더군

가만히 살펴보니 언젠가 당신이 흩뿌린 작은 꽃들이었어

나를 붙들고 진달래꽃 뿌리며 떼쓰던

당신도 함께 있더군

모른 척 돌아누웠지

당신이 있어서 정말 좋아

On a drizzly autumn morning

I was tossing and turning and there they were, others doing the same

As I closely looked at them, they were the petite flowers you had scattered
once

Amongst them, there you were too

You who had grabbed and whined at me, scattering azaleas at me

I turned over, pretending to know nothing

I am so happy that you are here.

연미복을 입은 베짱이

a penguin suited grasshopper

A penguin suited grasshopper struts to the main entrance

He started to render a mellifluous melody after nodding sweetly

to the audience

How astonishing!

It was truly mellow as it was the one that I played for so long in my heart

"Welcome to this sunlight flooded summer nation" said the grasshopper.

연미복을 입은 베짱이가 멋진 스텝을 밟으며 대문으로 들어섰어
달콤한 눈인사를 던지고 감미로운 선율을 연주하기 시작했어
놀라운 일이었어
오랫동안 마음으로 연주하던 선율이었거든
햇살 가득한 여름 나라에 오신 걸 환영해요 베짱이가 말했어

세상은 온통 말없는 말로 가득해

산 꽃 나무 냇물도 만 가지 말을 주고받나봐

말없는 말을 이해할 수 있다면 정말 행복할 텐데

문득 그녀 가슴에 귀 기울여 보았어 콩닥콩닥 소리가 들려와

이제야 알겠어 당신을 사랑해요 라는 말이라는 걸

The whole world is filled with soundless words

Mountains, flowers, trees and streams exchange countless words

I would be happy if I understood these soundless words

I listened carefully to the pounding of her heart: *Lub-dub, lub-dub*

I see now that this says 'I love you.'

산을 보면 가슴이 뭉클해

웃지도 울지도 않고 늘 같은 마음이잖아

뛰지도 걷지도 못하고 늘 같은 자리에 있잖아

새처럼 울고 꽃처럼 웃는 너를 보면 어느새 산이 되거든

산처럼 너른 가슴이 되거든

가슴이 뭉클해지거든

When I look at a mountain, my heart moves

It never laughs nor cries but simply remains the very same mind

It stands its ground, neither running nor walking

When I look at you, crying like a bird and laughing like a flower,

 I become a broad-hearted mountain

My heart moves.

벌거벗은 당신이 내게 왔을 때 부끄러움에 숨이 멎었습니다

나도 따라 벌거벗고 싶지만 용기가 없었습니다

망설이는 시간 속에 가을이 지나가고 나무들이 옷을 벗습니다

나도 절로 당신 앞에 옷을 벗습니다

사랑을 시작할 시간입니다

When naked you came, you took my breath away with shyness

I, too, wanted to be naked but was not bold enough

Autumn passed while I was hesitating and the trees started to take off their

clothes

Now, I too take off my clothes

It's time for love to begin.

얼음골 여우가 말했어

슬픈 이야기를 들려줄께

이곳이 처음부터 추웠던 건 아냐

졸졸 시냇물이 흘렀으니까

어느날 휘파람 소리가 들렸어 가르랑 나쁜 마음 좋은 마음 편을 가르랑

순식간에 물이 얼어붙었어 그리고 다시는 녹지 않았어

The fox from an ice valley said

"Let me tell you a sad story."

"It wasn't freezing cold like this at the beginning."

"There used to be a brook trickling."

"One day, we heard a whistling sound casting a spell – "Duro, Duro! Split into

a good spirit and split into an evil spirit."

Within a split second, the water froze up solid and never melt again.

마음 속에 독을 품었어 사불사불 독을 키웠어

사랑은 독이라는 걸 알아 퍼런 입술 물고 이대로 죽으려는데

되돌아 오는 당신 모습에 몸이 다시 살아요

독보다 천배나 지독한 당신 손길에 몸이 다시 붉어요

I bore poison in my heart and nurtured the poison – fang hiss fang hiss

Love is poison, yes, that's why I let myself die, biting my purplish lips

But looking at you returning, I am revived

Your touch – a thousand times more brutal than poison – heats me up, so

rubicund again.

검은 안경을 쓴 아이가 날 보고 있었어

검은 눈동자를 빛내며 아이가 말했어 꼭 해야 할 일이 있어요

까마득한 가슴 속으로 아이를 안아들였어

내가 당신을 사랑한 이야기를 세상에 전해야 해요

이제 사랑에 대한 이야기를 시작해야 해요

A child wearing dark glasses was looking at me

With his dark eyes sparkling, he said "There is something that I must do."

I lifted him up into my deep-seated heart

"I must let the world know about how I loved you so."

"Now I must start a story of love."

눈보라 치는 겨울날 참새 두 마리 날아왔어

오들오들 참새들을 품 속에 안았지

휘잉 눈보라를 바라보다 깜짝 품 속을 들여다보니

참새들이 눈처럼 녹아버린 거야

참새 두 마리 조잘조잘 품 속에 있으니 추운 겨울 따스하게 살아갈 거야

In a snowstorm, a pair of sparrows flew to me

Brrr, poor things, I held them in my arms

Whoosh, I looked at the snowstorm, then startled, I checked in the crook of

my arms

The sparrows had melted like snow

As long as the two birds are snuggled in my arms, twittering away, this cold

winter will be warm for me.

고래

a whale

became a whale wearing the sparkling sun as armour and rising straight up

I saw you on the beach, playing like a child

Your joyful laughter followed me even into my dreams

I held you in my belly and fell asleep

Even having become a deserted island, I am not lonely anymore.

고래가 되었어 번쩍이는 햇살을 갑옷처럼 입고

수직으로 솟구치는 고래가 되었어

해변에서 아이처럼 놀고 있는 너를 보았어

깔깔거리는 웃음이 꿈 속까지 따라왔지

배 안에 너를 품고 쿨쿨 잠들어 버렸어

무인도가 되었지만 더 이상 외롭지 않아

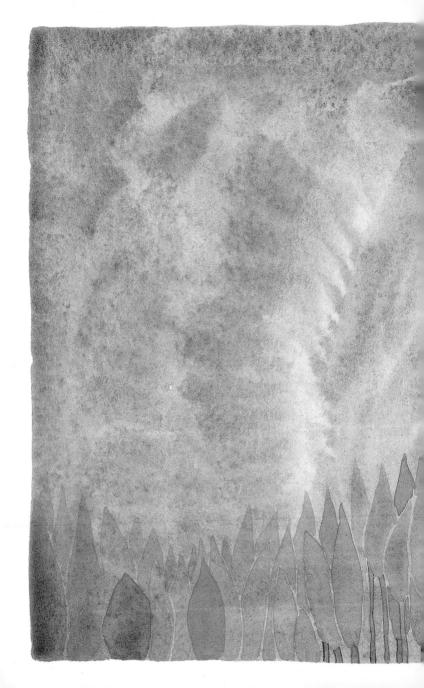

숲 속으로 들어갔지
수군거리는 소문으로 분주하더군
거기서 너를 만났지 진한 빛깔의 열매를 달고 나를 바라보더군
가끔씩 생각하네 수상한 의혹으로 가득한 세상에 대하여
거이한 확신으로 가득한 사랑에 대하여

I walked into a forest

It was busy with murmuring gossip

I found you there, looking at me with richly-coloured fruit hanging from you

Sometimes I think about a world full of quizzical doubts

About the kind of love which is full of peculiar certainties

진주가 태어나는 걸 보았어요

냄새 나는 작은 방이었어요

몸부림 치는 당신을 보다 눈물이 고였어요

눈물 속에서 영롱하게 빛나는 당신이 보여요

흐물거리던 몸이 단단해져요

눈물 가득한 사랑이 아니었다면 진주를 얻을 수 없었을 거예요

I have seen pearls being born

It was in a small, malodorous room

My eyes were filled with tears as I watched you struggle and flay

In this scene of tears, I see you sparkling brilliantly

I see your wobbly body turning rock-solid

Without all that tear-drenched love, perhaps it would have been impossible

for us to have a pearl.

호랑이를 만났어

화등잔처럼 큰 눈을 뜨고 날 보았어

아버지의 커다란 눈이 떠올랐어

등을 길게 편 호랑이가 꼬리를 높이 세우고 주변을 맴돌았어

어흥 하는 소리에 번쩍 깨어났고 화악 등잔에 불이 켜졌어

맑은 세상이 눈에 보였어

I met a tiger

He was staring at me with his big eyes - like an oil lamp

It was reminiscent of my dad's big eyes

The tiger, with his slender back and tail high up, hovered around me

"ROAR!", I awoke startled and the oil lamp flared brightly

I could then see it, a pure world.

하늘 밑 땅 위에 그가 살아요

이제 울지 않아요

가슴 속 멍울을 말없이 견디더라구요 머잖아 봉오리가 터질 거예요

화들짝 피어날 거예요 천 개의 산에서 꽃봉화가 오를 거예요

어린 사랑이 어른 사랑으로 변할 거예요

믿음으로 사랑을 기다려요

He lives on the ground, under the sky

I don't cry anymore

The million buds in me bore and forbore. These buds will explore soon and

bloom in full

Flowery beacon fires will rise from thousands of mountains

A feeble love will turn into a mature love

I await this love in trust.

고래
a whale
8-5

머리가 하얀 할아버지가 마당에 서 계셨어

고개 숙여 예를 표하니 지팡이 하나 건네주셨어

지팡이에 파릇파릇 이파리 돋아나더니 집채만한 나무가 자라났어

코훌쩍 눈물 훔치며 영차 까치발로 나무의 품에 안겼어

집채만한 나무와 사랑에 빠졌어

There was an old grey-haired man standing in the garden

Paying homage to him with a bow, he gave me a walking stick

A leaf sprouted from the stick and it grew into a huge tree

Sniffling and wiping away my tears, Heave-ho! Tippy-toed, I ran up to the tree

I fell in love with this monumental tree.

고래
a whale
8-6

I met you in a pitch-black room

You lit the lantern and looked at me with that luminous light

You uncovered the secret of the sparkling world; where tears transform into oil

Cha-ruu-ruu, when you light the lantern, *Hwa-ruu-ruu,* the day breaks

As tears are everywhere, so is oil

Heaven and Earth will finally have their daybreak.

캄캄한 방에서 너를 만났어

초롱에 불켜고 초롱초롱 나를 보았지

눈물을 기름으로 바꾸는 초롱 나라의 비밀을 알아냈구나

차르르 초롱불 밝히면 화르르 동이 틀 거야

눈물이 지천이니 기름도 지천일 거야

마침내 천지에 새벽이 올 거야

창가에 앉아

by the window

늦은 밤 창가에 앉아 당신을 기다렸지

창밖에는 회오리 바람 지나가고 당신은 바람 뒤에 계셨지

화들짝 뛰어나가니 바람의 손이 열어놓은 대문 안으로

세월의 바람 달고 계신 당신이 들어오셨지

집채만한 바람 가슴에 안으며 당신 품에 안겼지

I had been waiting for you by the window late at night

A whirlwind passed and I saw you standing behind the wind

As I jump out, you enter the main gate – opened by the wind's hand –

holding the winds of time

My heart, engulfed by these massive winds, I rushed into you.

Growl! I howled out in anger and chased away my tears

Hidden behind this flaming anger is the sound of weeping, writhing as it

fades away

As you came into my life and cast a spell - Abracadabra - everything changed

Flames turned into flowers, and tears revealed their bare pistils

Growl, a naked love has begun.

컹컹 화를 내어 울음을 쫓았지

불꽃처럼 피어나는 화 속에는 몸부림치며 사그라드는 울음이 있더군

네가 나타나 사부라다 주문을 외우니 모든 게 변했어

불꽃이 꽃으로 변하고 울음이 벌거숭이 꽃술을 드러내더군

컹컹 벌거숭이 사랑을 시작했지

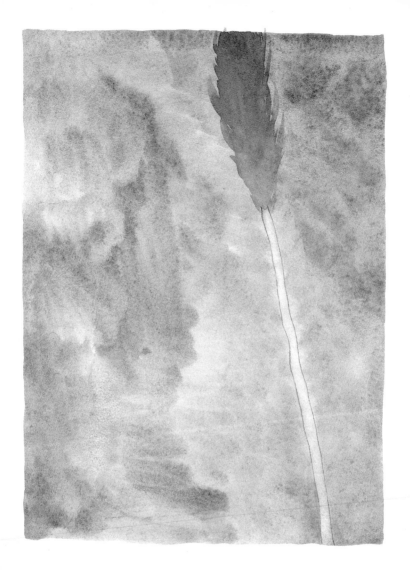

나무가 말했어 좋은 일이 있을 거야

나무가 말을 하다니

그럴 지도 모르겠는걸

나무가 웃음 지으며 말했어 천년에 한번 나무가 사랑에 빠지면

천지에 봄이 오는 거야

그럴 수도 있겠는걸

마침내 나무가 울상을 지으며 말했어

널 사랑한다구

A tree uttered, "Something good will happen"

How bizarre that a tree can talk

"Maybe it is possible."

The tree said with a smile, "When a tree falls in love once in a thousand years,

spring comes to Heaven and Earth."

"Maybe it is possible."

Finally, the tree spoke out, almost about to cry,

"I love you!"

빛 바랜 사진 속에서 웃고 있는 당신을 만났어

웃다가 눈물 번지며 당신이 말했지 여기서 그만 헤어져야겠어

사진 속에 손을 넣어 당신 손을 부여잡았어

그렇게 사진 속으로 걸어들어갔지

사랑 사진관의 쇼윈도우에 우리 사진이 걸려 있더라구

I met you – smiling in the faded photo

You said with a tearful face after laughing "Now, it's time to say good bye."

I reached into the photo with my arm and grabbed your hand

Just like that, I walked into the photo

Our photo hangs there, in the show window of the *Photo Studio Love.*

용이 나타났어 하얀 수염을 휘날리며

내게 말했어 때가 왔어 다른 세상으로 가야 해

울상이 되어 대답했어 하지만 어떻게 해야 할 지 모르겠다구

용이 사라졌어

하늘을 올려다보며 목놓아 울었어

용이 다시 나타났고 이번에는 내가 사라져버렸어

A dragon appeared before me with his whiskers fluttering

"Time is up. We have got to move onto the next world."

I answered back in tears, "I honestly don't know what to do."

The dragon disappeared

I looked up to the sky, melted into tears

the dragon has reappeared but I have vanished this time.

처음부터 그랬던 건 아냐

조금씩 달라져 갔어

남몰래 발가락이 뿌리로 변했지

칡뿌리 되어 땅 속으로 내려갔지

처음부터 그랬던 건 아냐

한달음에 달라져 버렸지

이제 큰뿌리되어 네 발 밑에 있어

차라리 땅이 되어 널 받들고 있어

It wasn't like this from the beginning

It changed gradually

My toes turned into roots without anyone noticing

They turned into arrowroots and plunged themselves down into the Earth

It wasn't like this the first time

It changed in the blink of an eye

Now being a big root, I'm under your feet

I am even the Earth, holding you up.

창가에 앉아
by the window
9-7

검은 눈동자 속에 어둠이 있어요

어둠 속에서 길을 찾아요

손을 꼭 잡으며 당신이 말해요 눈물이 홍수처럼 밀려오면

눈물 길을 따라 어둠의 나라를 떠날 거야

펑펑 눈물이 쏟아지고 눈물의 엑소더스를 시작해요

희뿌연 새벽 하늘이 보여요

There is a darkness, deep within those brown eyes

I have been seeking a way out from this darkness

As you grab my hands firmly, you say "When the tears flood into us,

we shall follow the path of tears and leave this world of darkness"

We embark upon an Exodus of Tears as the tears pour down

I see the morning haze of the dawning sky.

큰 사람

a gigantic person

큰 사람을 만났어요

큰 하늘에 그림처럼 걸려 있어요

그림 속의 큰 사람이 말해요 인생은 슬픈 거란다

슬픔이 밀려와 눈물로 맺혀요

큰 눈물이 큰 사람의 허벅지에 뚜욱 떨어져요

큰 사람이 그림 밖으로 걸어나와요

인생은 아름다운 거예요

I met a gigantic person

He was hanging in the skies like a big painting

He said, "Life is full of sadness"

Such sadness surged up and formed into tears

A big tear dropped onto his thigh

He now is walking out from the painting

Life is a truly wondrous thing.

큰 사람
a gigantic person
10-1

긴 사람이 있어요

길게 드리운 오후의 햇살을 지고 긴 한숨을 쉬어요

짧은 마음으로 동그란 손바가지를 만들어요 긴 한숨을 담아둘 요량으로요

그대야 손사래치지만 햇살 버무린 한숨이 아련하지요

찰랑대는 한숨 위에 그대의 얼굴이 아른거려요

There is a long person

Putting on the prolonging afternoon-sunshine, I let out a long sigh

I make a rounded hand-bowl with my short mind – hoping to keep the long

sigh in it

You wave dismissively but the sigh mixed in the sunshine is yet so vague

Your face is hazy on the top of the sloshing sigh.

I crawled inside a pot

I was thankful for the sloshing dew

Looking into the jar, I found a toad looking up at me

So I looked right back at him

I was thankful for the sloshing dew

The toad had gone and I came out of the jar

My scales, dropping from me.

항아리에 들어갔어

찰랑이는 이슬들이 고마웠어

항아리를 들여다보니 두꺼비 한 마리 올려다보겠지

나도 두꺼비 마냥 녀석을 내려다보았어

찰랑이는 이슬들이 고마웠어

두꺼비가 사라졌고 나도 항아리를 나왔어

비늘을 떨구며 항아리를 나왔어

There was a time when I was like my father's greatest treasure

snuggled in his hands

Leaving behind a diamond named love,

he became a single drop of water and drifted into the sunlight

He sometimes comes back to my wet cheeks as shining teardrops –

as the teardrops of longing.

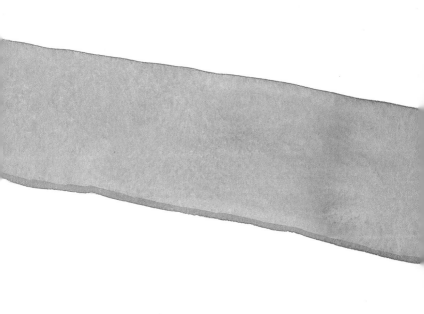

아버지 손에 쏘옥 들어가 금자동아 은자동아
그런 시절이 있었지
사랑이라는 이름의 다이아몬드를 남기고
물방울이 되어 햇살 속으로 날아가셨지
가끔씩 반짝이는 눈물 방울이 되어 축축한 내 볼에
다녀가시지 그리움으로 다녀가시지

I met an unknown woman

For some reason, I couldn't stop thinking of her

Just as I was about to lose my heart to her, I recalled you

That's why she seemed so oddly familiar

You are an unknown woman for me

Always meeting on a windy field

Always leading me into a glistening garden

You are a perpetually unknown woman.

낯선 여자를 만났어
자꾸만 마음이 가는 거야
선뜻 마음을 주려다 당신이 떠올랐어
어쩐지 낯이 익더라니까
당신은 낯선 여자야
언제나 바람부는 벌판에서 만나
언제나 햇빛 나리는 뜨락으로 인도하는
당신은 언제나 낯선 여자야

오래 기다렸어요

I waited so long for you

오래 기다렸어요

그리움이 대신 다녀갔지요

오잖을 줄 알았다면 그리움을 껴안았을 텐데요

꼭 오실 당신을 기다리느라 파고드는 그리움을 밀쳤답니다

당신은 오셨지만 저만치 뛰어가는 그리움이 이제는 안타깝네요

사무치게 그리웁네요

I waited so long for you

In lieu of you, the Longing came to me

If I knew that you were never going to return, I could have embraced the

Longing

But as I was so sure you would come, I pushed away the penetrating Longing

You have returned, but now I pity the Longing as it runs from me

The past is piercing my heart.

아침 햇살 아래 기골이 장대한 산이 말을 걸어왔어요

당신이었군요

언제부턴가 말을 걸어오는 사람이 있었는데

바로 당신이었군요

눈부신 햇살 아래 산의 품에 안겼어요

품이 너른 산이었어요

이제 눈을 감아야겠어요

A mighty mountain, bathed in fresh morning sunbeams started to talk to me

It was you

There has been someone striking up a conversation with me

I now know that it was you

I am wrapped in the mountain's arms under the stunning rays

of the morning sun

Such a spacious embrace the mountain gives

Now, I shall close my eyes.

On one truly thirsty afternoon, all I wanted was the offer of a bowl of water

But I am yet to meet the one offering

I am yet to encounter the *Nidana*, who, with a pure smile,

is kind enough to float a willow leaf in the water and hand it to me

It has become this thirsty moment,

yearning for a well of crystal-clear wind.

목마른 오후였네 물 한 바가지 얻어 마시고 싶지만

그런 사람 만나지 못했네

청초한 모습으로 미소 지으며 물 위에 버들잎 하나 띄워주는

그런 인연 얻지 못했네

청아한 바람 부는 우물가를 그리워하는

목마른 시간이 되어버렸네

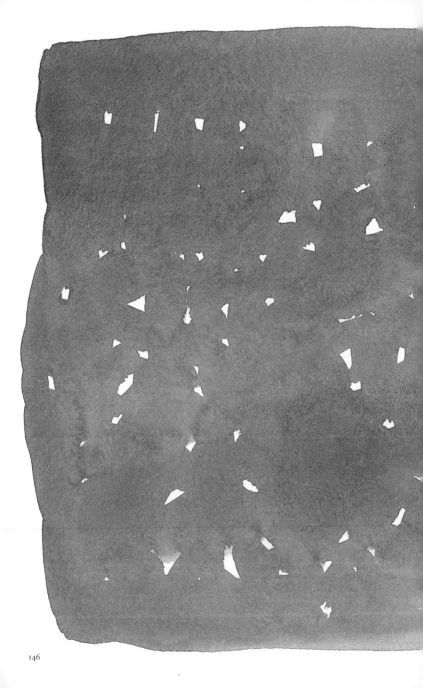

당신을 좋아하고부터 이런 생각 들었어요
눈송이보다 내가 더 소중할 까닭이 없구나
그런 생각 들고나니 눈송이 귓가에 스치며 속삭이더군요
네가 있어 참 좋아
온갖 생각 하다보니 눈송이 되어 당신 곁을 스치게 되었어요
당신이 있어서 좋아

No reason I should be more treasured than a single snowflake -

this thought has lingered since I first fell for you

Once this thought was out, a snowflake brushed my ears and whispered,

 "I love having you here."

As a million thoughts rush by, I become a snowflake, brushing right past you

"I love having you here."

Delicate vegetables came to my garden, adorned in sparkling morning dew

I bumped into them when I popped to the garden in the early morning

Without noticing, I had become one of them

I took the next step, and was served up at the breakfast table with them

After breakfast, I touched my arms and legs

I found them unscathed

It was odd.

반짝이는 이슬을 입은 여린 채소들이 우리집 텃밭에 왔더라구

이른 아침 밭에 갔다 그들과 마주쳤어

나도 모르게 그들과 하나되었지

내친 김에 아침 밥상에까지 올랐어

아침 상을 물리고 나서 팔다리를 만져보았지

멀쩡하더라구

신기한 일이었어

오래 기다렸어요
I waited so long for you
11-6

노란 새 한마리

까르르 날아올라요

웃는 소리인지 우는 소리인지 모르겠어요

세상을 지우고 녀석을 그렸어요

자기를 그린 걸 알았나 봐요

웃는 소리인 게 분명해요

새는 날아갔지만 녀석을 사랑하게 되었어요

노란 그리움이 와르르 내려앉아요

A yellow bird flew away

Tweet-tweet

I'm not sure if it is laughing or crying

I erased this world and drew a picture of him

He seemed to know that I was drawing him

Now I'm sure it was laughter I heard

The bird flew away but I had already fallen in love with him

Ah, this yellowish feeling of longing lands so heavily.

Two beauteous human beings are nodding

As one nods, the other nods too

Finally, as the two nod at the same time, the Earth nods too - swing, swing

I too, sit on a swing

Ding dong - the clock is ticking towards midnight

A beautiful new day is just dawning.

아름다운 두 사람이 고개를 끄덕여요
한 사람이 끄덕이면 또 한 사람도 끄덕여요
마침내 두 사람이 한꺼번에 끄덕끄덕 지구도 덩달아 끄덕끄덕 흔들려요
나도 따라 흔들그네를 타요
때앵 시계가 자정을 지나고 있어요
아름다운 새날이 밝아요

The immeasurable grief that countless people felt

Far from disappearing, it may have piled up somewhere and became

a noble creature

I dare to find him even if it means searching the entire universe

I shall only be able to part from these countless sorrows once I am in

his tender embrace, as loving as the morning dew.

수없는 사람이 느낀 수없는 슬픔은

사라지기는 커녕 어딘가에 쌓여 인간보다 고귀한 생명체가 되었으리라

우주를 뒤져서라도 그를 찾아내고야 말리라

아침 이슬처럼 다사로운 그의 품에 안기고 나서야

비로소 수없는 슬픔과 이별하리라

A butterfly flew to me

It was late at night

She was long and thin, flying grandly

She didn't look like she belonged to this world at all

Oddly, she was even smiling

I delicately sat on her back, longing to go to another world with her

It was a deep night.

나비 한 마리 날아왔어요

늦은 밤이었어요

키 큰 나비였어요 성큼성큼 날더라구요

이 세상 나비 같지 않았어요

방글방글 웃기까지 하더라구요

조심조심 나비 등에 올라탔어요 나비 따라 다른 세상으로 가려구요

깊은 밤이었어요